Pete the Cat

The Wheels on the BUS

By James Dean

HARPER
An Imprint of HarperCollins*Publishers*

Pete the Cat: The Wheels on the Bus

For information address HarperCollins Children's Books, a division of HarperCollins Publishers, 195 Broadway, New York, NY 10007.
www.harpercollinschildrens.com

Library of Congress Cataloging-in-Publication Data
The wheels on the bus / based on the creation of James Dean. — 1st ed.
p. cm. — (Pete the cat)
Summary: Pete the cat's school day is recounted in this twist on the classic song.
ISBN 978-0-06-219871-6 (hardcover bdg.)
1. Children's songs, English—United States—Texts. [1. School buses—Songs and music. 2. Schools—Songs and music. 3. Cats—Songs and music.]
I. Dean, James, date.
PZ8.3.W572 2013
782.42—dc23 2012014222
[E]
CIP
AC

The artist used pen and ink, with watercolor and acrylic paint, on 300lb hot press paper to create the illustrations for this book.
15 16 17 18 SCP 10 9 8 7

First Edition

To my mother and grandfather—Jeanette Brown Thomas and Paul Richard Brown:
Thank you for always being there and making sure we kids had everything we needed.

The wheels on the bus go round and round,
round and round,
round and round.
The wheels on the bus go round and round
all day long.

The horn on the bus goes beep, beep, beep,
beep, beep, beep,
beep, beep, beep.

The horn on the bus goes

beep,

beep,

beep

all day long.

The wipers on the bus go swish, swish, swish,
swish, swish, swish,
swish, swish, swish.

The wipers on the bus go swish, swish, swish
all day long.

BUS

The signals on the bus go blink, blink, blink,

blink, blink, blink,
blink, blink, blink.

B

The signals on the bus go blink, blink, blink
all day long.

BATTERY

The motor on the bus goes zoom, zoom, zoom,

zoom, zoom, zoom,

zoom, zoom, zoom.

The motor on the bus goes

zoom, zoom, zoom

all day long.

The door on the bus goes open and shut,
open and shut,
open and shut.

The door on the bus goes

open and shut

all day long.

LUNCH

LUNCH

The kitties on the bus say, "Come on, Pete!
Come on, Pete!
Come on, Pete!"

The kitties on the bus say,
"Come on, Pete!"
all day long.

The driver on the bus says, "Move on back!
Move on back!
Move on back!"

The driver on the bus says,

"Move on back!"

all day long.

Pete's friends on the bus say, "Sit with us!
Sit with us!
Sit with us!"
Pete's friends on the bus say,
all day long.

Sit with us!

LUNCH

The back of the bus bumps up and down,
up and down,
up and down.
The back of the bus bumps up and down
all day long.

BUS

The kitties on the bus go

Pete the Cat,

Pete the Cat,

Pete the Cat.

The kitties on the bus go

Pete the Cat

all day long.

The dog on the bus goes woof woof woof,
woof woof woof,
woof woof woof.

The dog on the bus goes

woof woof woof

all day long.

The cats on the bus shout,
"Let's rock out!
Let's rock out!"

The cats on the bus shout,

"Let's rock out!"

all day long.

BUS

The wheels on the bus go round and round,
round and round,
round and round.
The wheels on the bus go round and round
All day long.

All day long.

All day long.

Pete the Cat

Old MacDonald Had a Farm

by James Dean

HARPER
An Imprint of HarperCollins*Publishers*

Pete the Cat: Old MacDonald Had a Farm

 For information address HarperCollins Children's Books, a division of HarperCollins Publishers, 195 Broadway, New York, NY 10007.
www.harpercollinschildrens.com

ISBN 978-0-06-219873-0 (trade bdg.)

The artist used pen and ink, with watercolor and acrylic paint, on 300lb hot press paper to create the illustrations for this book.
Typography by Jeanne L. Hogle
14 15 16 17 18 SCP 10 9 8 7 6 5 4
❖
First Edition

Old MacDonald had a farm, E-i-e-i-o!
And on that farm he had some chickens, E-i-e-i-o!

With a cluck-cluck here,
And a cluck-cluck there,
Here a cluck, there a cluck,
Everywhere a cluck-cluck,
Old MacDonald had a farm,

E-i-e-i-o!

Old MacDonald had a farm, E-i-e-i-o!
And on that farm he had some dogs, E-i-e-i-o!

With a **woof-woof** here,
And a **woof-woof** there,
Here a **woof**, there a **woof**,
Everywhere a **woof-woof**,
Old MacDonald had a farm,

E-i-e-i-o!

Old MacDonald had a farm, E-i-e-i-o!
And on that farm he had some cows,
E-i-e-i-o!

With a Moo-Moo here,
And a Moo-Moo there,
Here a Moo, there a Moo,
Everywhere a Moo-Moo,
Old MacDonald had a farm,

E-i-e-i-o!

Old MacDonald had a farm, E-i-e-i-o!
And on that farm he had some pigs, E-i-e-i-o!

With an oink-oink here,
And an oink-oink there,
Here an oink, there an oink,
Everywhere an oink-oink,
Old MacDonald had a farm,

E-i-e-i-o!

Old MacDonald had a farm,

E-i-e-i-o!

And on that farm he had some horses,

E-i-e-i-o!

With a **neigh-neigh** here,
And a **neigh-neigh** there,
Here a **neigh**, there a **neigh**,
Everywhere a **neigh-neigh**,
Old MacDonald had a farm,

E-i-e-i-o!

Old MacDonald had a farm,

E-i-e-i-o!

And on that farm he had some cats,

E-i-e-i-o!

With a meow-meow here,
And a meow-meow there,
Here a meow, there a meow,
Everywhere a meow-meow,
Old MacDonald had a farm,

E-i-e-i-o!

Old MacDonald had a farm,

E-i-e-i-o!

And on that farm he had some goats,

E-i-e-i-o!

With a baa-baa here,
And a baa-baa there,
Here a baa, there a baa,
Everywhere a baa-baa,
Old MacDonald had a farm,
E-i-e-i-o!

Old MacDonald had a farm, E-i-e-i-o!
And on that farm he had some ducks,

E-i-e-i-o!

With a quack-quack here,
And a quack-quack there,
Here a quack, there a quack,
Everywhere a quack-quack,
Old MacDonald had a farm,

E-i-e-i-o!

Old MacDonald had a farm, E-i-e-i-o!
And on that farm he had some turkeys,
E-i-e-i-o!

With a gobble-gobble here,
And a gobble-gobble there,
Here a gobble, there a gobble,
Everywhere a gobble-gobble,
Old MacDonald had a farm,

E-i-e-i-o!

Old MacDonald had a farm, E-i-e-i-o!
And on that farm he had some roosters,
E-i-e-i-o!

With a cock-a-doodle here,
And a cock-a-doodle there,
Here a cock-a-doodle,
there a cock-a-doodle,
Everywhere a cock-a-doodle,
Old MacDonald had a farm,
E-i-e-i-o!

Old MacDonald had a farm, E-i-e-i-o!
And on that farm he had some donkeys,
E-i-e-i-o!

With a hee-haw here,
And a hee-haw there,
Here a hee-haw, there a hee-haw,
Everywhere a hee-haw,
Old MacDonald had a farm, E-i-e-i-o!

Old MacDonald had a farm, E-i-e-i-o!
And on that farm he had some sheep, E-i-e-i-o!
With a maa-maa here,
And a maa-maa there,
Here a maa, there a maa,
Everywhere a maa-maa,
Old MacDonald had a farm, E-i-e-i-o!

Old MacDonald had a farm,
E-i-e-i-o!
And on that farm he
had some frogs,
E-i-e-i-o!

With a ribbit-ribbit here,
And a ribbit-ribbit there,
Here a ribbit, there a ribbit,
Everywhere a ribbit-ribbit,
Old MacDonald had a farm,

E-i-e-i-o!

Old MacDonald had a farm, E-i-e-i-o!
And on that farm he had some geese, E-i-e-i-o!

With a **honk-honk** here,
And a **honk-honk** there,
Here a **honk**, there a **honk**,
Everywhere a **honk-honk**,

Old MacDonald had a farm,

E-i-e-i-o!

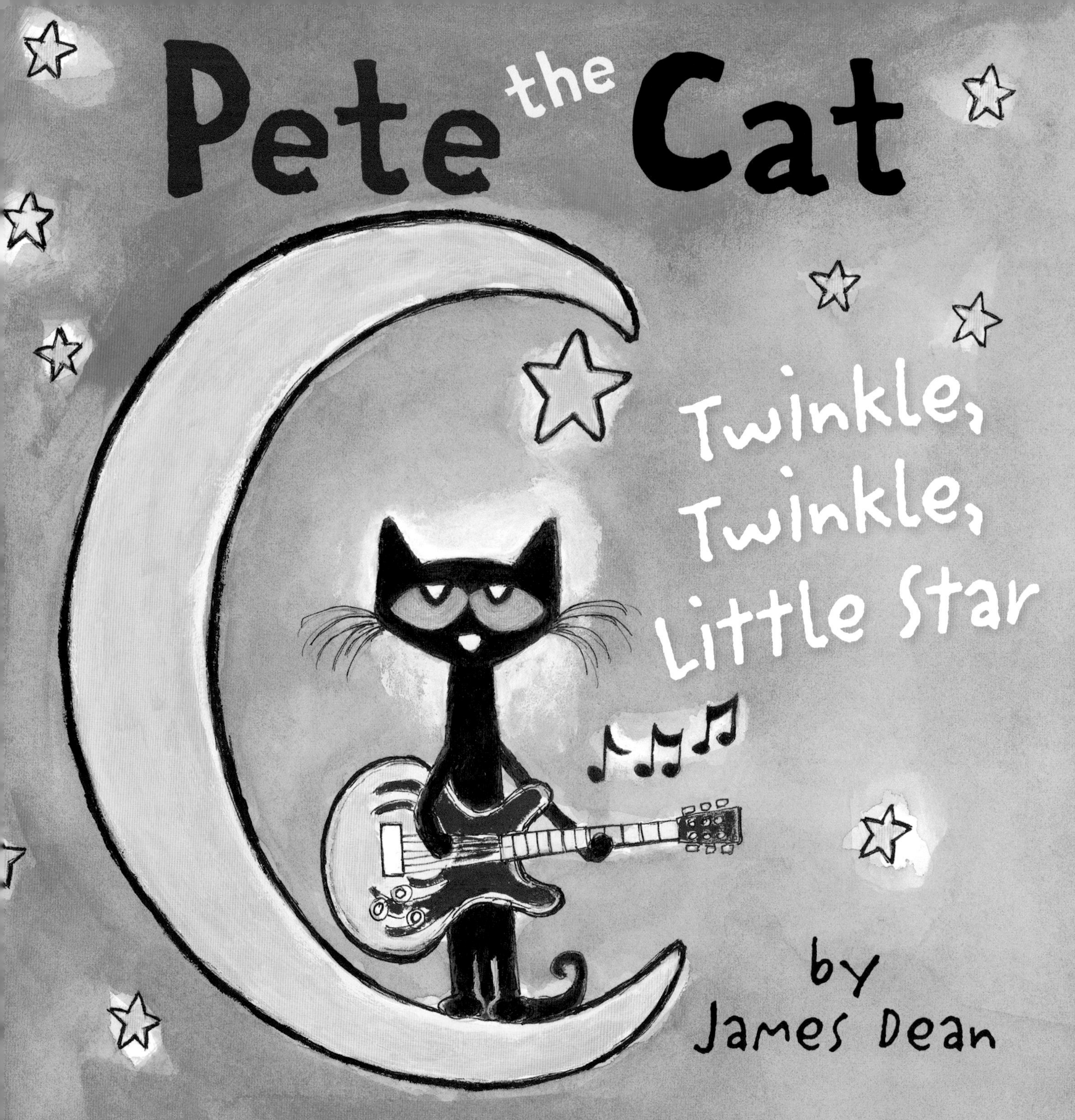

HARPER
An Imprint of HarperCollins*Publishers*

Pete the Cat: Twinkle, Twinkle, Little Star

For information address HarperCollins Children's Books, a division of HarperCollins Publishers, 195 Broadway, New York, NY 10007.
www.harpercollinschildrens.com

ISBN 978-0-06-230416-2

The artist used pen and ink, with watercolor and acrylic paint, on 300lb hot press paper to create the illustrations for this book.
Typography by Jeanne L. Hogle
14 15 16 17 18 SCP 10 9 8 7 6 5 4

First Edition

Twinkle,
twinkle,
little star,

How I wonder what you are!

Up above the world so high,

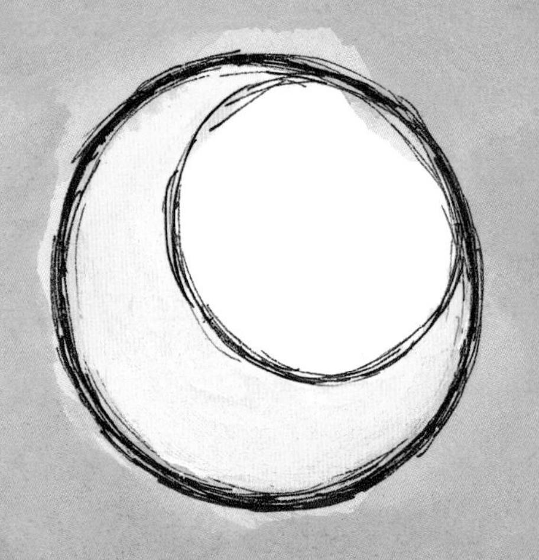

Like a diamond in the sky.

When the blazing sun is gone,

When he nothing shines upon,

Then you show your little light,

Twinkle,
twinkle, all the night.

Then the traveler in the dark,
Thanks you for your tiny spark.

Spelling Words:
cat
meow
dog
paws
whisker
mouse
Litter

He could not see which way to go,
If you did not twinkle so.

In the dark blue sky you keep,
And often through my curtains peep,

For you never shut your eye,
Till the sun is in the sky.

As your bright and tiny spark,
Lights the traveler in the dark.

Though I know not what you are,
BEDTIME STORIES for CATS
The CAT and the FIDDLE

Twinkle,
twinkle,
little star.

BEDTIME STORIES for CATS
The CAT and the FIDDLE

How I wonder what you are!

Up above the world so high,
Like a diamond in the sky.

Twinkle,
twinkle,
little star,

How I wonder what you are!

How I wonder what you are!